AUG   2017

PUDDLES!!!

Kevan Atteberry

 KATHERINE TEGEN BOOKS

An Imprint of HarperCollins Publishers

Hey, Laura! Hey, Patrick! Hey, Bryan!

Hey, Del! Hey, Mims! Hey, Bevvers! Hey, Lynn!

Hey, Whatsits!

Hey, Tighty Writeys!

Look at me!

Katherine Tegen Books is an imprint of HarperCollins Publishers.

Puddles!!!
Copyright © 2016 by Kevan Atteberry. All rights reserved. Manufactured in China. No part of this book may
be used or reproduced in any manner whatsoever without written permission except in the case of brief
quotations embodied in critical articles and reviews. For information address HarperCollins Children's Books,
a division of HarperCollins Publishers, 195 Broadway, New York, NY 10007. www.harpercollinschildrens.com

ISBN 978-0-06-230784-2

The artist used Adobe Photoshop to create the digital illustrations for this book.
Typography by Erica De Chavez.
16 17 18 19 20 SCP 10 9 8 7 6 5 4 3 2 1
❖ First Edition

Hello, sun.

Hello, clouds . . .

Rain! Rain! Rain!

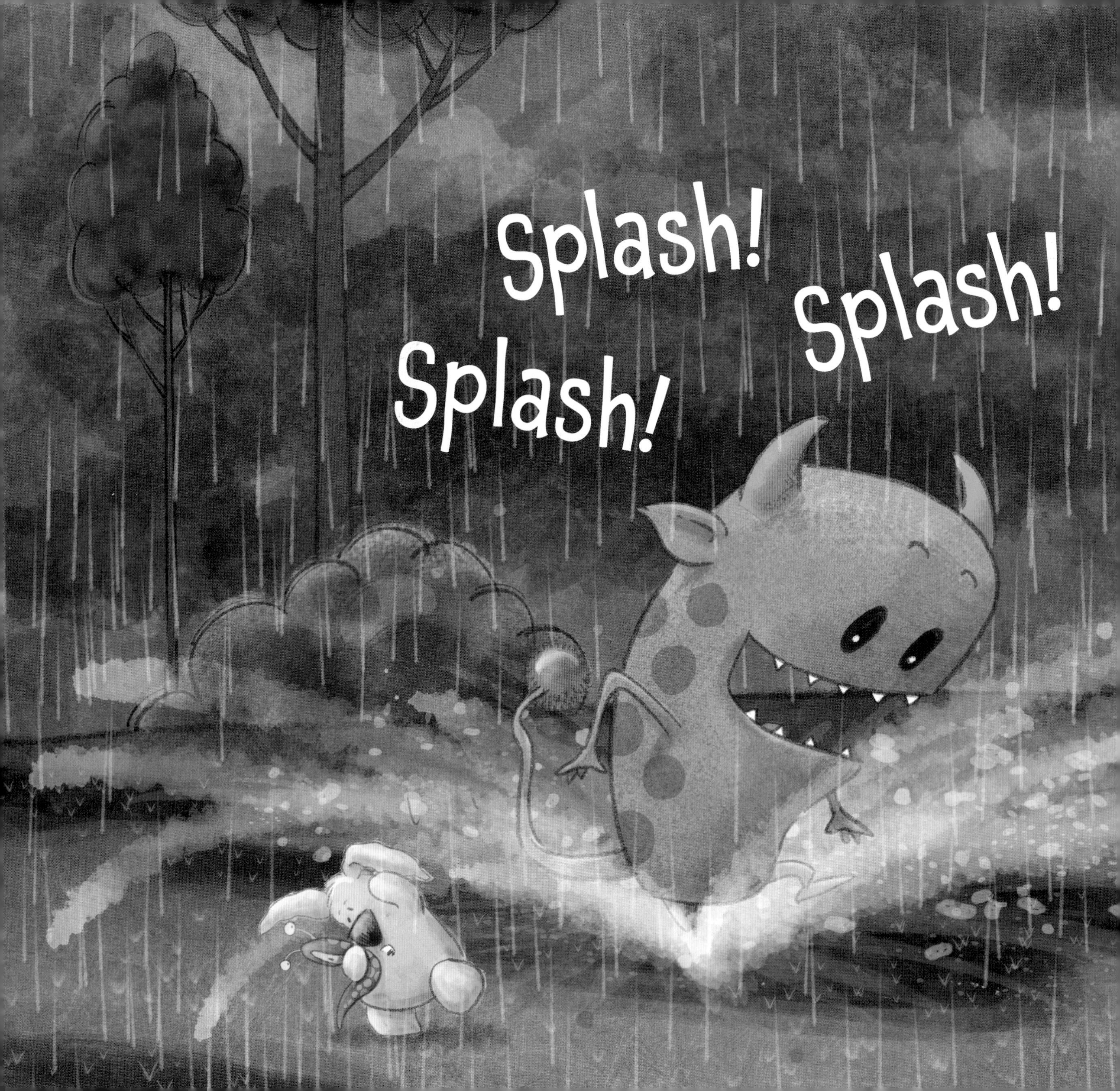
Splash!
Splash!
Splash!

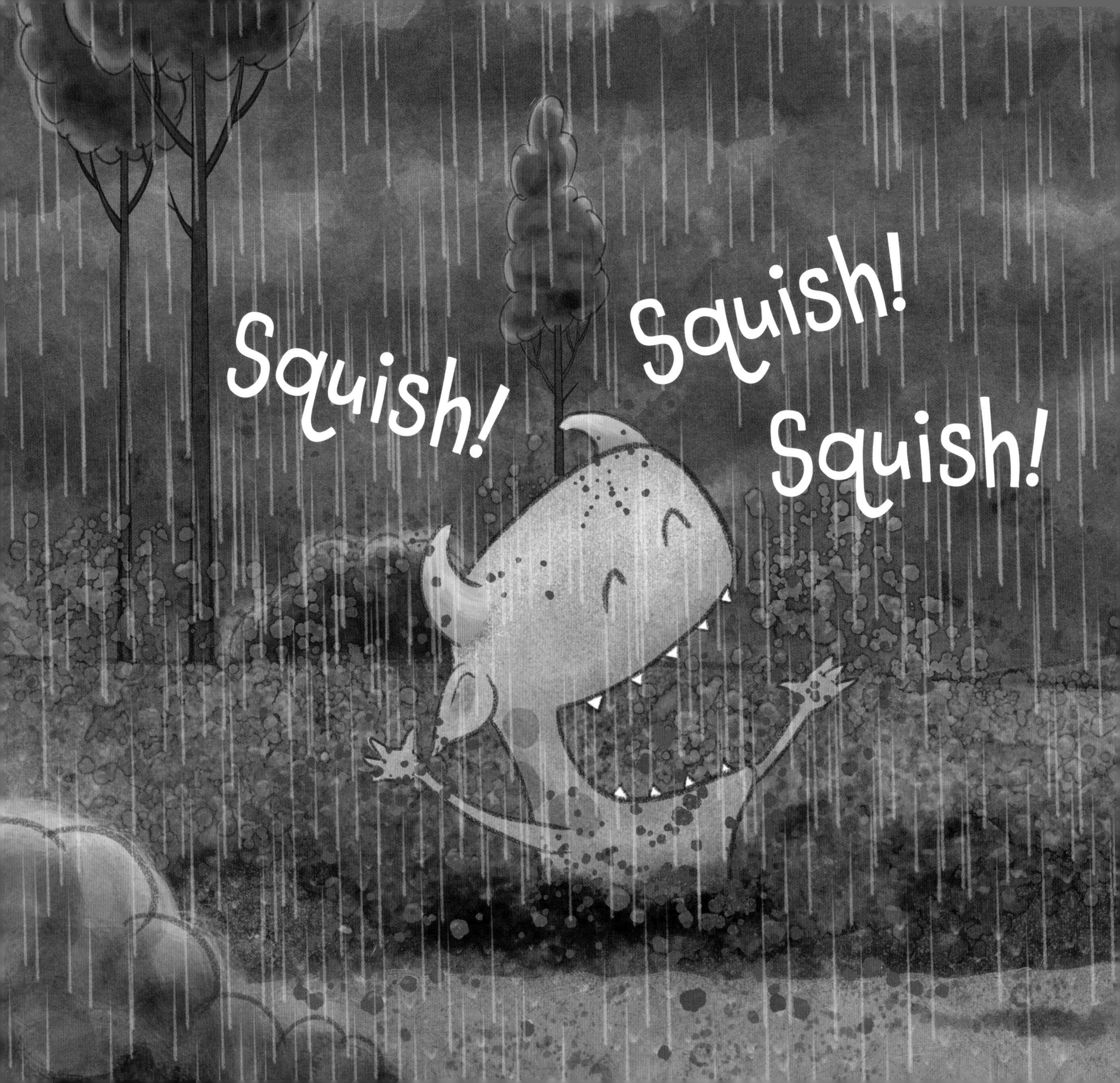
Squish!
Squish!
Squish!